GIRLS ROCK!

Snowball Attack

Jacqueline Arena

illustrated by
Lloyd Foye

RISING STARS

First Published in Great Britain by
RISING STARS UK LTD 2006
22 Grafton Street, London, W1S 4EX
Reprinted 2008

For more information visit our website at:
www.risingstars-uk.com

British Library Cataloguing in Publication Data
A CIP record for this book is available from the British Library.

ISBN: 978-1-84680-060-3

First published in 2006 by
MACMILLAN EDUCATION AUSTRALIA PTY LTD
15–19 Claremont Street, South Yarra 3141

Visit our website at www.macmillan.com.au or go directly to
www.macmillanlibrary.com.au

Associated companies and representatives throughout the world.

Series created by Felice Arena and Phil Kettle
Project management by Limelight Press Pty Ltd
Cover and text design by Lore Foye
Illustrations by Lloyd Foye
Printed in China

UK Editorial by Westcote Computing Editorial Services

GIRLS ROCK!
Contents

Rachel   Ellie

CHAPTER 1

Snow Way!

It's the school holidays and Ellie is really excited. She picks up the phone and calls her best friend, Rachel.

Ellie "Hi Rachel. What are you up to?"

Rachel "I'm playing 'Alpine Skiing' on my PlayStation. What's up?"

Ellie "Forget about playing. You can do it for real."

Rachel "What? What are you talking about?"

Ellie "Have you been outside today?"

Rachel "No way, it's too cold. Ellie, what's going on? You sound really excited. Did you win a year's supply of books or something?"

Ellie "Ha, ha, really funny. No, look outside your window. You're not going to believe it!"

Rachel "Don't tell me, it's like the film we saw the other day—the one where people look out their windows and see that they're being invaded by aliens in tutus."

Ellie "Rachel! Just go and look."

Rachel wanders over to her bedroom window with the phone.

Rachel "Wow! I don't believe it. It's snowing right outside my window. The whole street is covered in snow. How did that happen? We've never had snow here."

Ellie "I know! Snow! Beautiful, flaky snow."

Rachel "Wow! It's everywhere."

Ellie "I just heard the weatherman on the TV. He's going crazy."

Rachel "This is so cool. Come over."

Ellie "Just try stopping me. See you soon."

CHAPTER 2

Snow Angels

Within minutes Ellie is at Rachel's house.

Ellie "This is so amazing."

Rachel "I know. Feel it. It looks so good—I could eat it!"

Ellie "Me, too. My Mum said it hasn't snowed here for nearly a million years."

Rachel "Yes, when dinosaurs wore snow boots and earmuffs!"

Ellie "Well, they wouldn't have worn anything because it would have been the ice age—and that's when they all died out. Except for mammoths and creatures like that."

Rachel "Er, Earth to Ellie—I was joking."

Ellie "Oh. I knew that."

Rachel "Hey Ellie, I'm going to make a snow angel."

Rachel lies on the snow-covered grass and swings her arms and legs. She stands up to have a look at her creation.

Rachel "Cool!"

Ellie "That's so beautiful, Rachel. I'm going to do one, too."

Ellie has a turn at making a snow angel. She struggles to swing her arms and legs at the same time. She hops back onto her feet to take a look.

Rachel "Hmm. It's ... er ... nice."
Ellie "Yes, if it was a snow rhinoceros."

Both girls laugh.

CHAPTER 3

Splat!

Suddenly, out of nowhere, *splat!*
splat!—Ellie and Rachel are hit in the
back by two snowballs.

Ellie "AAAGGGHHHH!"
Rachel "Who did that?"

Rachel turns to see her neighbours, Jim and Tim, peeking over the fence.

Rachel "I should have known it was them. The evil brothers."

Ellie "Look out! They're throwing some more!"

Two more snowballs shoot over the fence towards the girls.

Rachel "We're being attacked! Duck!"

Rachel throws herself on the ground, pushing Ellie down, too. Ellie gets a face full of snow. Her glasses are covered in ice.

Rachel "Are you okay, Ellie?"

Ellie (spits out snow) "Yes, I should have worn my snow glasses."

Rachel "You have snow glasses?"

Ellie "Er, Earth to Rachel—I was joking."

Rachel "Oh. I knew that."

The girls stand up and brush the snow off themselves.

Rachel "I think they've gone."

Ellie "Good. Let's make a snowman."

Rachel "What? Are you serious? We've got to get the boys back!"

Ellie "Really?"

Rachel "Er ... yes!"

Rachel and Ellie trudge to the front of Jim and Tim's house. Snow continues to fall.

Ellie "Rachel, what are you doing?"

Rachel picks up a handful of snow and shapes it into a ball.

Rachel "Knock on the door, Ellie,
and then step aside quickly so
you're out of the way."

Ellie "Rachel, you're not going to do
what I think you're going to do?"

Rachel "Hurry up, Ellie, my
snowball's melting. Knock on the
door and then when the boys open
it up—*wham, splat!*"

Ellie taps on the door.

Rachel "Knock louder, Ellie. They'll never hear."

Ellie "Are you sure this is a good idea? Here goes nothing."

Ellie knocks hard on the door and steps aside. As the door opens, Rachel throws the snowball as hard as she can.

Splat!!!

Rachel makes a direct hit, but not on the boys. The snowball hits the boys' father!

CHAPTER 4

Snow March

The girls apologise to their neighbour. Fortunately, he smiles and tells them that the boys are sledging down a hill in the park at the end of their street.

Rachel "Let's go."
Ellie "Where?"

Rachel "You heard him. The boys are at the park."

Ellie "Rachel, forget about getting them back. Let's make some really cool snow sculptures instead."

Rachel walks back to the side of her house and grabs two plastic dustbin lids.

Ellie "Now what are you doing?"

Rachel hands one of the lids to Ellie.

Rachel "You'll see."

The girls walk towards the park down the end of their street.

Rachel "Get ready for combat, Ellie."

Ellie "Now I know what we're going to do. We're going to use these as sledges, aren't we?"

Rachel marches a few steps in front of Ellie.

Rachel "You'll see."

Ellie and Rachel reach the park and quickly duck behind a tree. They see the boys at the top of the hill about to slide down.

Rachel "Here, Ellie. Hold this for a second."

Ellie (whispering) "What are we doing? Why aren't we sledging?"

Rachel "We're not here to sledge."

Rachel bends down and makes a snowball.

Ellie (holding up the bin lids) "Then what did we bring these for?"

Rachel hands the snowball to Ellie and then makes one for herself.

Rachel "When the boys make it down to the bottom, that's when we attack."

Ellie "Attack? But, but …"

Rachel "Quick, here they come."

Ellie "But what about these bin lids?"

Rachel "Just do what I do. OK, ready, charge!"

CHAPTER 5

Take That!

Rachel and Ellie run out from behind the tree, taking the boys by surprise. Rachel throws her snowball and it hits one of the brothers.

Rachel "Yes! Take that! Throw yours, Ellie."

Ellie tosses her snowball. *Splat!* It hits the other brother.

Rachel "Nice one, Ellie!"
Ellie "Thanks! I didn't think I could throw that well. Uh-oh, look out!"

The boys quickly make snowballs and throw them back at the girls.

Rachel "Hold up your lid, Ellie!"
Ellie "What?"
Rachel "Like this!"

Rachel holds her bin lid in front of her and stops the snowball mid-flight.

Ellie "Oh, now I get it! They're shields."

Rachel "Ellie, look out!"

Ellie lifts her lid up to her face just in time—a snowball splats against it.

Ellie "Yikes, that was close!"

The girls continue to throw snowballs at the boys. A few minutes later the boys give up and run home.

Rachel "Yes! Yes! We got them!"

Ellie "That was such a cool idea, Rachel!"

Rachel "Of course it was. Snow's always cool—get it?"

Ellie "That's a really bad joke."

Rachel "Snow way!"

Ellie "That's worse."

Rachel "Are you calling me a flake?"

Ellie (giggling) "Stop it!"

Rachel "I thought I was being so n-ice to you."

Ellie "Can we build that snowman now?"

Rachel "Yes, do you know what they eat? Icebergers!"

Ellie "Oh Rachel, bad joke!"

As the snow continues to fall, Rachel tells bad snow jokes all the way home.

Ellie "Stop! Stop! No more jokes! I can't take it!"

Rachel "But I'm just warming up … after the snow I mean."

Ellie "Hey Rachel, let's go back to your place and have hot chocolate with marshmallows."

Rachel "Yes, I'm ready to chill out big style!"

Rachel

GIRLS ROCK!

Snow Lingo

Ellie

blizzard When heaps of snow falls and you can't see anything in front of you except snow.

condensation When water vapour in the air turns into liquid (if the liquid freezes, it's snow).

snow angel A figure you make in the snow by lying on your back and moving your legs and arms back and forth.

snowball champion Whoever makes the best snowballs … and aims them at the best target!

sledge Something you sit on to slide in the snow. You steer it by shifting your weight from side to side.

GIRLS ROCK!

Snow Must-Dos

☆ Wear gloves when you make snowballs—otherwise, your fingers might freeze and fall off.

☆ Keep an eye out for dustbin lids when you play in the snow—you never know when you'll need a shield to protect yourself from snowballs.

☆ Make sure that when you aim a snowball at someone, you hit your target—and not their Dad or Mum!

☆ If you fall down while you're learning to ski, just keep smiling and say, "I meant to do that".

☆ Before you make a snow angel, check to make sure there's no dog poo in the area.

☆ If your fingers start to turn blue, get inside and drink some hot chocolate to warm up!

☆ Don't assume that white specks on somebody's shoulders are dandruff—it might just be snow.

☆ If you've never seen snow, go rent a snowy movie such as "The Snowman" or "The Chronicles of Narnia" and pretend that you're there.

GIRLS ROCK!

Snow Instant Info

❄ Snowflakes form when water vapour in the air cools and turns into drops of water. Each drop then freezes into a tiny ice crystal smaller than the full stop at the end of this sentence.

❄ Snowflakes are like fingerprints— no two are exactly alike.

❄ The first sledges were long, flexible, narrow and pulled by hand. They were made of bark and animal skin and used to haul stuff over the snow.

❄ Early skis were not made for speed, but were designed to keep a traveller on top of the snow as they went about their business.

❄ The greatest snow storm in North America occurred in February 1959 when 4.8 metres of snow fell in a single storm at Mt. Shasta Ski Bowl in California, USA.

❄ Canada holds the record for the most snow angels made at the same time, but in different places. Sixty different schools made 15,851 snow angels simultaneously.

❄ The largest snowman on record was 34.6 metres tall. His eyes were made of Christmas wreaths, his mouth was made of six car tyres and each arm was a 3-metre-tall tree.

Think Tank

1 What is the common name for ice crystals?

2 What's the best protection against snowballs?

3 What were the first sledges made of?

4 How do you make a snow angel?

5 What's the main ingredient of a snowball?

6 What was used for the mouth of the biggest snowman on record?

7 What do you see in a blizzard?

8 Were the earliest skis designed for speed?

Answers

1 The common name for ice crystals is snowflakes.

2 The best protection against snowballs is a good dustbin lid.

3 The first sledges were made of bark and animal skins.

4 You make a snow angel by lying on your back and moving your arms and legs back and forth in the snow.

5 The main ingredient of a snowball is snow, of course!

6 The mouth of the biggest snowman on record was made of six car tyres.

7 You see nothing but snow in a blizzard.

8 No, the earliest skis were designed to keep people on top of snow.

How did you score?

- If you got all 8 questions correct, you could study at university to become a snow scientist.

- If you got 6 answers correct, think about becoming the snow reporter on the TV in a really snowy place like the North Pole or Antarctica.

- If you got fewer than 4 answers correct, have fun using dustbin lids as protection against water balloons rather than snowballs.

Hey Girls!

I hope that you have as much fun reading my story as I have had writing it. I loved reading and writing stories when I was young.

Here are some suggestions that might help you enjoy reading even more than you do now.

At school, why don't you use "Snowball Attack" as a play and you and your friends can be the actors. Get some cotton wool to use as snow, screwed-up balls of paper for snowballs and two dustbin lids. These will be your props. So ... have you decided who is going to be Ellie and who is going to be Rachel? And what about the narrator?

Now act out the story in front of your friends. I'm sure you'll have a great time!

You also might like to take this story home and get someone in your family to read it with you. Maybe they can take on a part in the story.

Whatever you choose to do, you can have as much fun reading and writing as a bee in a honey jar!

And remember, Girls Rock!

Jacqueline Sarina

GIRLS ROCK!
When We Were Kids

Jacqueline *Holly*

Jacqueline talked with Holly, another *Girls Rock!* author.

Jacqueline "Did you grow up with snow?"

Holly "Yes. When it snowed, we listened to the radio to find out if school was closed."

Jacqueline "Why did your school close?"

Holly "Because buses couldn't move in the snow, so we couldn't get there."

Jacqueline "Brilliant. Did you play in the snow all day?"

Holly "Yes. What about you? What was your favourite snow activity?"

Jacqueline "Wearing sunglasses while I ate a cherry-flavoured ice cream!"

GIRLS ROCK!
What a Laugh!

Q What did the singing snowman say to the actor?

A There's no business like snow business!

GIRLS ROCK!

The Sleepover

Pool Pals

Bowling Buddies

Girl Pirates

Netball Showdown

School Play Stars

Diary Disaster

Horsing Around

Newspaper Scoop

Snowball Attack

Dog on the Loose

Escalator Escapade

Cooking Catastrophe

Talent Quest

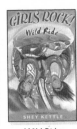
Wild Ride

Camping Chaos

Mummy Mania

Skater Chicks

GIRLS ROCK! books are available from most booksellers. For mail order information please call Rising Stars on 0870 40 20 40 8 or visit www.risingstars-uk.com